PORTSMOUTH PUBLIC LIBRARY
175 PARROTT AVENUE
PORTSMOUTH,
603 427 1540

D0560457

# Hey Jack! Books

First American Edition 2012
Kane Miller, A Division of EDC Publishing

Text copyright © 2012 Sally Rippin
Illustration copyright © 2012 Stephanie Spartels
Logo and design copyright © 2012 Hardie Grant Egmont
Design by Stephanie Spartels
Typesetting by Michaela Stone
First published in Australia in 2012 by Hardie Grant Egmont

All rights reserved, including the rights of reproduction
in whole or in part in any form.

For information contact:
Kane Miller, A Division of EDC Publishing
P.O. Box 470663
Tulsa, OK 74147-0663
www.kanemiller.com
www.edcpub.com
www.usbornebooksandmore.com

Library of Congress Control Number: 2012931653

Printed and bound in the United States of America
3 4 5 6 7 8 9 10
ISBN: 978-1-61067-122-4

# Hey Jack!

# The Scary Solo

By Sally Rippin

Illustrated by Stephanie Spartels

**Kane Miller**
A DIVISION OF EDC PUBLISHING

# Chapter One

This is Jack.

This morning Jack is in a jittery mood. He wants to try for a solo in the school concert.

Jack likes singing,
but he feels too shy
to try out by himself.
So he has asked his
best friend Billie
to stand with him
while he sings.

Billie and Jack
practice singing in the
playground. They are
going to be **stars**!

"Next, please," calls Miss Winters. She is in charge of the school concert. Today she is choosing children for the solo parts.

Now it is Jack's turn to try out for a part.

Jack walks onto the stage.

4

Billie follows and stands next to him.

Jack gets ready to sing.

But all of a sudden Jack feels nervous and wobbly. He hops from one foot to the other like he has **ants in his pants**.

The music starts. Jack
knows all the words,
but when he opens his
mouth, nothing comes out!

Jack stands with his mouth
wide-open. His tummy
squeezes tight.

Billie pokes him
in the ribs. "Hey, Jack!"
she says. "What's wrong?"

Jack closes his mouth.

It's no use. He is much

too **scared**

to sing on his own.

He feels silly

for even trying.

Miss Winters smiles kindly.
"Perhaps you can be
in the chorus, Jack.
Now, Billie, are you
trying out too?"

Billie nods. The music
starts, and Billie sings
loudly and clearly.

Jack feels cross and
sad at the same time.
He wishes he was
as brave as Billie.

"Well done, Billie!" says Miss Winters when Billie has finished. "You can have a solo. You sing very well."

Billie jumps up and down in excitement.

Jack frowns. *But I can sing too!* he thinks crossly. *I can sing as well as Billie! It's just that...*

10

11

Jack sighs. He hangs his head as he and Billie leave the hall.

# Chapter Two

Billie runs out into the playground. Jack mooches along behind her.

"I can't believe it!" says Billie. "I got a solo!"

All the kids in the playground stand around Billie and cheer for her.

Jack can see that Billie
is happy. He wants
to be happy too.
But right now he just
feels **cross**.
It was *his* idea to try out
for a solo in the school
concert. Not Billie's!

Jack scrunches up his
face and kicks the ground.

He feels a big, dark
monster inside him
grumbling to be let out.

16

"It's only a stupid school concert!" Jack shouts. "Who wants to sing a solo anyway? Only stupid people!"

Billie turns to Jack. Her mouth drops open, and her eyes grow wide.

"Jack!" she says. "That's mean!"

Jack knows it's mean.
But he can't help it.
It's the big, grumpy
monster talking, not him.

Jack runs away from
Billie to the other end
of the playground.

For the rest of the day,
Jack and Billie don't
speak to each other.
Jack glares at Billie,
and she glares back.

Jack wants Billie to
say sorry. He doesn't
know why.

It's not fair that she got a solo in the school concert and he didn't.

But soon the **grumpy** monster in Jack's tummy goes away. He knows it is up to him to say sorry.

"I'm sorry for being mean," he says. "I'm happy that you got a solo, Billie. Really. Friends?"

"Friends," Billie says, smiling. "Forever."

"Hey, maybe you can help me practice my solo?" Billie adds.

Jack nods. "Sure," he says.
"I'd like that."

All that week and
the next, Jack helps
Billie practice her
solo for the musical.

They sing everywhere.
In the kitchen and in the
bathroom. In the backyard
and in the house.

23

24

They sing as loud as
rock stars – except when
it's time for Billie's
baby brother to have
a nap. Then they sing
baby Noah to sleep.

Jack can't wait for
the concert!

# Chapter Three

Finally the day of
the school concert
arrives. Jack and Billie's
families drive to the
school hall.

Billie and Jack are both wearing shiny silver tops. This is the costume their class is wearing for the concert.

Billie also has glitter in her hair. She looks just like a rock star.

Jack feels a teensy bit **jealous** when he sees Billie's hair. He wishes he had a solo too. He knows being in the chorus is an important job, but it's not as exciting as being a solo singer.

"Good luck, Billie!"
their parents shout
excitedly. "Hey, Jack!
Good luck!"

Billie and Jack
wave to their
parents. They
run backstage.
Jack skips
with excitement.

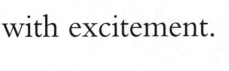

Soon it's time for
the concert to begin.

Every class is doing
a different song in
the concert. Jack and
Billie wait with their
class until it is their
turn to go on stage.

They wait and they wait.
Everyone is nervous
and **giggly**.

Sometimes Miss Winters
pokes her head into the
back room and frowns.

"Shhh!" she says
with her finger on
her lips. But this
just makes everyone
giggle even more.

Jack and Billie
practice their song
very quietly together.

Only two more songs,
and they are on!

Jack feels his tummy
flipping like a fish.

"OK!" Miss Winters whispers to Jack's class. "You're up next!"

Everyone in Jack's class runs onto the stage and stands in their positions. Billie stands in front, ready to sing her solo.

"Go, Billie!" Jack whispers.

The curtains open.

The music starts.

The spotlight shines
on Billie. Everyone
waits for her to sing.

Billie lifts up her
microphone. Her
mouth opens. But no
sound comes out!

*Oh no!* Jack thinks.

35

He knows *exactly*
what's wrong with Billie.
He knows that her legs
will be **wobbling**
like jelly.

The music stops.
Everybody looks at Billie,
waiting… waiting…

*Poor Billie!* thinks Jack.
*She has no one to help her!*

Billie is still standing
at the front, frozen.

*Wait a second*, thinks Jack.
*I know this solo!*

He runs to stand
next to Billie. Then he
grabs the microphone
and holds it between
himself and Billie.
He begins to sing.

The music starts
up again. Jack sings
loud and strong.
He knows all the words
by heart.

Billie stands with
her eyes wide-open.

Still singing, Jack
jabs her with
his elbow. He looks
at her and smiles.

Finally, she starts
to sing too. Quietly
at first, but then
louder and louder.

Soon Jack and Billie are singing at the top of their voices. Just like at home.

When Jack and Billie's class has finished the song, everyone claps and cheers.

People **Stomp**
their feet on the ground
and shout, "More! More!"

Jack and Billie's
parents cheer the
loudest of all.

Jack's smile stretches
across his face.
He looks at all those
cheering people.

41

He feels a big warm
burst of sunshine
in his chest.

He is a star!

43

# Collect them all.